Her grandchildren are far, far away and she misses them terribly, but nothing discourages Grandma or can keep her away. Follow her adventures as she hides in more and more improbable places.

"Hidden Grandma" is part of the *I Love My Grands* series.

Hidden Grandma

Susan Riehle

Library of Congress Cataloging-in-Publication Data

Riehle, Susan Author & Illustrator

Hidden Grandma / Susan Riehle—1st ed.

ISBN: 9798408691319

Dedication

To my sister, my kids, my grandkids,
and the real Grandpa, who is far nuttier
than the fictional one.

Chapter 1
Grandma

My Grandma lives so far away
And sometimes I wish she could come and stay
Each time I beg, "Come home with me!"

"With you, imagine what our lives would be!"
The dog and cat might notice first:
In that suitcase there are more than just shirts!

With a soft whine and a loud purr
Then a reply of "Shush" and oddly smoothed fur

Chapter 2
Changes

Over time, the dog and cat grew fatter

Purrr.....purrrrrr

Purrr.....purrrrrr

Purrr.....purrrrrr

And I thought I knew what was the matter!

Baby never slept through the night
Now she goes off to bed without a fight
All morning she smiles discretely

What's the secret she's keeping so sweetly?
She giggles, "Ga ga ma" with glee
It's obvious! Am I the only one who sees?

Chapter 3
Not just the kids!

Snort
Snort
Hrumpt
Wheeze
Snorrre
Snort
Snort
Hrumpt
Zzzzzz
Zzzz
Zzzz
Hmmm
Zzzz
Zzzzz
Zzz...hmmm
Zzzz
Zzz

Mom and Dad sleep later I find
Snoring loudly, no worry crosses their mind

The house seems to order itself

Could this just be a kindly...er...elf?

"No way, it just couldn't be?"

But what else could it be…I don't know, let's see?

Brother and I suspect the cause
And start a house-wide search without pause

Chapter 4
Could it be?

We searched closets and pantry
Checked garage, doghouse, and entry

We heard a familiar giggle

Off to the side we thought we saw a wiggle

Sights and sounds only half-seen
Stuff was here and there, but then suddenly clean

This hidden grandma is clever
But not even she could hide forever

Chapter 5
Outside too

Outside, too, things changed for some reason
Garage and yard, she hid, through several seasons

In Spring, she befriended some old pals

Who hid her between them with hidden smiles

In Summer, she frolicked in trees

In Fall, she blended in cleverly with the leaves

In Winter, Santa was surprised to know

They shared a chimney and rooftop, covered in snow

Chapter 6
Love

Oh, she wasn't perfectly neat
We noticed she trailed things so sweet
We found her under the hamper—hooray!

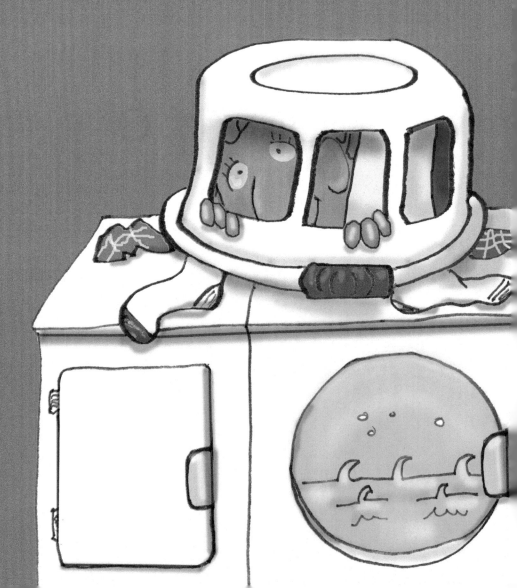

We hugged and frolicked so much
Then asked dear Grandma
"What's this, what's up?"

She smiled, "I couldn't stay away"
"It was harder and harder each day"

It will happen, I know it will, again
Hidden Grandma is oh, oh, oh so much fun

Brother and I kept her secret and play'd
We enjoy her hide and seek game each day

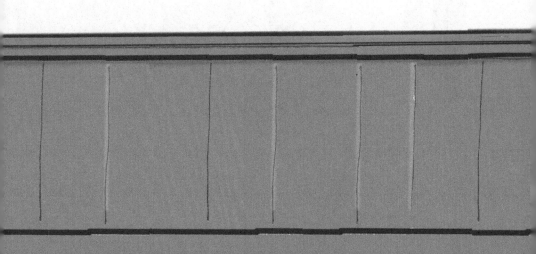

Chapter 7
The end

She'll visit whenever we say
It's clear that nothing can keep her away
It's our little secret—it's true

…but next time please:
"Can Grandpa come too?"

My Grandma and I like to...

Garden

Read books together

Act silly

Nibble on fresh-baked treats

Draw and paint

Make crafts

Act like adults

        & dance

Make up stories

Enjoy movies together

About

Susan Riehle is a mom, engineer, cartoonist, business-owner, and play-on-the-floor type of grandmother. Her books celebrate love, individuality and creativity.

Look for more adventures of Grandma and Grandpa in the *I Love My Grands* series.

Susan's personal mission is to strengthen families. If you like this book, please review it!

Adventures with Grandpa

Join Grandpa on his madcap adventures as he explores a world fueled by imagination, whimsy, and laugh-out-loud wackiness. (Obviously, age is not a guarantee of maturity!)

In his first story he fantasizes he is a superhero only to accidentally become one in real life. Grandpa books are part of the *I Love My Grands* series.

I Love My Grands

A Fun With Grandma & Grandpa Book

Made in the USA
Coppell, TX
12 October 2022

84485046R10044